READ ALONE *Get set with Read Alone!*

This entertaining series is designed for all new readers who want to start reading a whole book on their own.

The stories are lively and fun, with lots of illustrations and clear, large type, to make first solo reading a perfect pleasure!

Other titles in the Read Alone series:

Rebecca Taylor

The Kitnapping of Mittens

Illustrated by Mark Southgate

VIKING

To Hannah and Mittens

VIKING

Published by the Penguin Group
Penguin Books Ltd, 27 Wrights Lane, London W8 5TZ, England
Viking Penguin, a division of Penguin Books USA Inc.,
375 Hudson Street, New York, New York 10014, USA
Penguin Books Australia Ltd, Ringwood, Victoria, Australia
Penguin Books Canada Ltd, 2801 John Street, Markham, Ontario, Canada L3R 1B4
Penguin Books (NZ) Ltd, 182–190 Wairau Road, Auckland 10, New Zealand

Penguin Books Ltd, Registered Offices: Harmondsworth, Middlesex, England

First published 1991
10 9 8 7 6 5 4 3 2 1

Filmset in Linotron Times by Rowland Phototypesetting Ltd,
Bury St Edmunds, Suffolk

Printed in Great Britain by
Butler & Tanner Ltd, Frome, Somerset

A CIP catalogue record for this book is available from the British Library

ISBN 0–670–83424–6

Contents

1.
The Woman in Black

Late one night, Mittens was feeling bored. She looked across at Hannah, her friend, who was fast asleep on a chair in the kitchen. Their owners had shut them in before they went to bed. But Mittens noticed they had forgotten to shut the cat-flap. She suddenly felt excited at the thought of the dark garden. She would go out! She would see what it was like at night! She knew that Hannah would be angry when she found out in the morning because she had told Mittens firmly that she was not allowed out alone at night. But Mittens had had enough of being treated like a little kitten. She was only going into the garden and that was not very dangerous. Mittens crept over to the door, every now and then looking at Hannah to see if she was still asleep.

Then she leapt through the cat-flap *very* quickly indeed.

Hannah stirred in her sleep, dreaming of catching mice, but did not wake up. She had no idea what danger little Mittens was in!

Meanwhile, Mittens had got

down to the bottom of the garden. She was about to sit down to have a rest, when she heard a strange rustling noise in the bushes.

"That's funny!" thought Mittens. "It's not like anything *I've* ever heard!"

She peered into the bushes and saw a strange woman. She was dressed in black and wore a black pointed hat and cloak and held a broom. She was turning stones over and peering into the holes that they had made. Suddenly, she dipped her hand down and brought out a fat toad. Cackling, she put it quickly into her pocket.

"This looks like an interesting game," thought Mittens. "Perhaps I can join in." And without further

thought she walked up to the woman.

"Hello!" said the woman. "What a pretty little kitten you are!" She began to stroke Mittens, who purred happily. "Do you want to come and live with me?"

Mittens looked at her eyes and thought, "She looks very kind."

Without warning, she felt herself being lifted up and then she drifted off to sleep. The woman was a witch and she had put a spell on her!

When Mittens woke up, she found herself in a kind of

cavern, lying next to a big
black pot. There was no sign of
the witch and it was still
night-time. She sat up and
stretched herself. Then she
began to wash her fur. When

she had finished, she went to
look outside. She saw nothing
but trees, trees, trees all
around her. She didn't like the
look of things and thought
she'd better not go out. Mittens
turned and went back into the
cavern. She looked in disgust
at the frogs, toads and spiders
that hopped and crawled
about. She peered into the pot
but could not make herself
drink any of the stuff, though
she was very thirsty. The liquid
was a deep purple and puffs of
smoke arose from its depths.
Presently, the witch came back.
"Hello, pussy," she said,

smiling at the little cat.
"What's your name then? You didn't tell me, did you?"

Mittens said (in cat language): "My name is Mittens."

"That's a pretty name, isn't it?"

Mittens stared at her in surprise.

"What's the matter then?" the witch asked impatiently. "Has a dog got your tongue?"

Mittens found her voice and said, "I didn't think human beings could understand us talking!"

"Ah well, I can!" said she.

"But I am not like other
humans. I'm a witch!"

Mittens leapt back,
frightened.

"Don't be afraid. I won't
hurt you. Anyway, do you

want some tasty mice for your
supper? There's no fancy cat
food around here!"

"Oh yes, please!" said
Mittens, in delight.

"And there's a little stream
near here if you want a drink.

There it is over there, you see?"

"Yes," said Mittens happily.

"And when you've had that I'll show you how to be a proper witch's cat. And the first thing you'll need to learn is how to ride on my broomstick!"

2.
The Cats' School

Meanwhile, Hannah had woken up in the morning and found Mittens gone. She was very worried. Then she noticed the cat-flap was open.

"Oh no!" she thought. "Mittens must have disobeyed me and gone out alone into the night!"

"I should have looked after

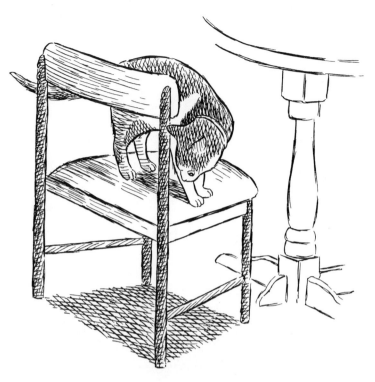

her better," said Hannah
guiltily to Whiskers, her friend,
later.

"Don't worry!" replied
Whiskers. "She'll turn up
soon."

But Hannah couldn't help
worrying.

"Come on, we'll be late for school!" said Whiskers.

The school was held in some old stables in a nearby garden. Hannah and Whiskers arrived

rather late. On the way to their lesson they saw a class of young cats with Mr Sunny, looking at the paw prints of a fox. Others were being taught to climb trees by Miss Leo.

Then they found their own group in the barn behind the stables where Miss Tibs was teaching them how to catch mice and other small animals.

"Sorry, Miss Tibs!" Hannah said to her, apologetically.

"I should hope so!" said Miss Tibs, sternly. "Please set a better example next time!"

"Yes, Miss Tibs," chorused Hannah and Whiskers.

At break, the other cats in Hannah's class crowded around her and Whiskers.

"Why were you so late? What's happened?" everyone demanded.

"I'm only going to tell
Smokey and Melinda,"
Hannah answered, firmly.
They were her other two best
friends.

25

She pulled them into a corner.

"Well, the secret is . . ."

Hannah stopped and looked at her friends.

"Go on, quick!" exclaimed Melinda.

"Well, Mittens has disappeared!"

"Oh dear, how dreadful!" cried Smokey. "Have you any idea where she might be?"

"No, not a clue," said Hannah, miserably. "She just vanished without a trace."

"Oh, what are we going to do?" said Melinda, helplessly.

"I'm going to look for her,"

Hannah decided.

"But you can't!" cried
Melinda. "You don't know
where she's gone."

"I'll ask my friend, Winnie
Wildcat, if she has seen Mittens
anywhere."

"Well, go after dinner, because there's stewed mice and rat delight and you don't want to miss that, do you?" said Smokey.

Hannah licked her lips, but shook her head.

"I must rescue Mittens first, Smokey. Mittens is more

important than food!"

"Well, if you're sure . . ."
began Melinda.

"Oh, I am!" interrupted
Hannah.

"If you're sure, you'd better
take a bottle of water and
some blackbird sandwiches
with you, because you'll

probably be hungry and thirsty and so will Mittens," continued Melinda.

"Yes, I'll do that!" said Hannah.

Smokey got all the things and put them in a rucksack. Hannah set off down the road. "Bye," she called.

"Good luck," said Melinda and Smokey, waving. They watched her until she was a speck in the distance. Turning, they padded thoughtfully back to school.

3.
Hannah's Journey

Hannah walked for some time. She came to the big forest and went in, looking for her friend, Winnie Wildcat, amongst the trees. Hannah finally found her eating the remains of a bird in her den, which was a big, roomy cave.

"Hello, Winnie," said Hannah. Winnie looked up, in surprise.

"Oh hello, Hannah," she said. "What are you doing here? I would have thought you'd be at school!"

"Well, I was," answered Hannah. "But Mittens is missing and I'm looking for her."

"Who is Mittens? Oh, do you mean that little rascal of a

kitten that you have to live
with?"

Hannah eyed her coldly.
"Yes, I do," she said. "But you
don't have to call her names,
you know!"

"Oh, sorry!" said Winnie, hastily. "I just forgot for a moment that she was a friend of yours."

"Anyway," said Hannah, "I came to ask you if you'd seen

her anywhere last night."

"Now, let me see . . . There were a few cats prowling around . . . and there *was* a little one that looked a bit like Mittens, now I think about it."

"Where?" said Hannah, eagerly.

"Erm . . . She was with a witch, flying on a broom!"

Hannah stared in dismay. "Which way were they flying?" she asked.

"Towards Spooky Wood. There *is* a witch that lives there, I believe, right in the middle."

"Oh no!" exclaimed

Hannah. "It sounds scary, but I'm still going on! I can't leave poor Mittens with a witch!"

"You are *brave*!" said Winnie, admiringly.

"No I'm not! It's just that, if Mittens is in danger, well, I've got to rescue her. It's my duty, and besides, I like her very much. She's a nice little kitten and that's a fact!"

"Oh, before you go, I'll catch you some mice for the journey, because it's a long way to Spooky Wood from here."

"Thanks a million. You *are* a good friend," said Hannah.

Winnie tied two large mice on
to Hannah's collar.

"Well, bye, then!"

"Goodbye and good luck,"
said Winnie.

Hannah went along quickly

now, fearing that Mittens
might have been hurt in some
way.

She soon came out in the
open. There was Spooky Wood
in the distance. After a while,
Hannah reached the wood and
went in. It seemed to her that
lots of eyes were peering at her

from the bushes and trees. She shivered. There was a rustling noise nearby. Hannah looked around, fearfully. Then she shook herself. "Don't be so silly!" she said.

Suddenly, a strange, bright light appeared in front of her. It hovered in the air. Hannah arched her back and hissed. Gradually, a figure emerged from the light. It was a fairy.

"Don't be afraid!" said the fairy. "My name is Lily. I'm here to help you. I've heard you are journeying to rescue your friend from the witch. Everyone in Spooky Wood hates her so we would be grateful if she was defeated. But you may find yourself in danger. There are dragons in this wood. If you meet one, give him these dragon sweets because dragons love them. Say that if he will promise to let you by, then he can have them."

"Thank you, Lily," said Hannah. "I'll do exactly as you say. Goodbye."

"Goodbye," said Lily. And she vanished.

Hannah continued on her way, looking left and right for any possible dragons.

Presently, there was a great
roaring noise and some smoke
came drifting towards her.
When it cleared, she saw a
dragon! She tried to run away,
but it was no use. The dragon

had her tail in his talons!
Hannah turned round and
faced him. He was really quite
small for a dragon.

"It must be a young
dragon," thought Hannah.

"What do you want?" he said, in a booming voice which echoed around the wood. Hannah was very frightened, but she tried not to show it. Then she remembered the dragon sweets and felt better.

"Please, sir, I've come in search of my friend, Mittens, who I think has been captured by the witch of Spooky Wood."

"Well, I could help you, but I'm rather hungry."

He looked at her, meaningfully. Again, Hannah was scared, but said hurriedly:

"Well, actually, I've got a present for you."

"What is it?" he asked.

"It's some dragon sweets," Hannah said, boldly. "But you can only have them if you let me by!"

"Ooh! Lovely! I haven't tasted dragon sweets for decades. If you give me them, I'll give you directions to the witch's cave and take you part of the way, too!"

"*Thanks a lot*, Mr Dragon!" said Hannah, in delight. She gave him the sweets and they set off.

It was now getting dark, so Hannah suggested that they find a place near a stream to

sleep for the night. This they
did, and settled down. They
drank from the stream and
Hannah ate one of the mice
while the dragon ate some of
the sweets.

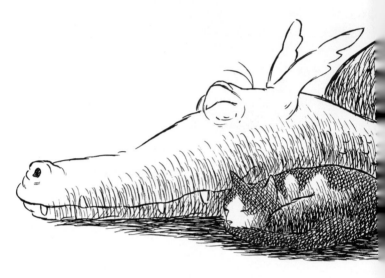

"Oh, by the way," said Hannah, "you didn't tell me your name. What is it?"

"My name's Flame. What's yours?"

"Hannah."

"That's a nice name, isn't it?"

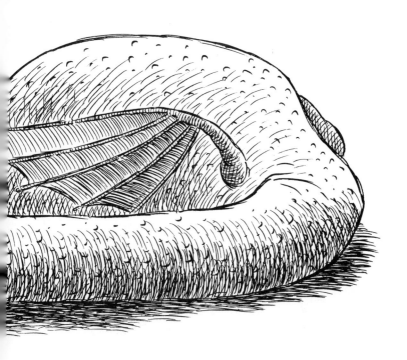

"Yes, I like it very much myself. Well, good night then."

"Good night," said Flame, sleepily. And with that, he fell fast asleep. Hannah lay awake for a while, gazing at the stars. Then she, too, fell asleep.

4.
Hannah to the Rescue!

The next morning, feeling refreshed after their long sleep, they continued their journey.

After a while, Hannah began to get a bit tired, so Flame said:

"It would be quicker to fly. Do you want to, Hannah?"

"Thanks, Flame. Are you sure it won't cause you any trouble?"

"No, no trouble at all! Your body's very light to me."

Hannah felt relieved. She tried to climb on to Flame's back, but it was too high. So Flame put his tail on the ground and Hannah climbed up that way. She clung on tightly as they rose into the air. The only sounds she could hear

were Flame's powerful wing
beats. Suddenly, there was
silence. Hannah opened her
eyes and looked down at the
ground below. She gasped. "If
I fall . . ." Hannah thought.

Towards midday, Flame flew

down to earth for a rest and
Hannah caught some more
mice to eat. After lunch, Flame
said:

"I think I'll have to go back
now. Mum has said that I
mustn't go too near the witch's
cave."

"Oh, Flame, do you have to go?" said Hannah sadly.

"Yes, I'm afraid I do. I'm rather busy this afternoon," replied Flame, hastily. "But you're not far from the witch's cave and perhaps I'll see you again sometime!"

"Yes, that would be nice," said Hannah, cheering up a little.

The dragon, preparing to fly, spread his wings. Turning, he said affectionately, "Bye, Hannah."

"Bye, Flame," said Hannah. As she went on her way, she said to herself, "Flame seemed rather afraid. I wonder if all dragons are scared of witches?"

Soon she came to the witch's cave. She hid in some bushes to wait for night to fall. Then she heard the witch say,

"Now I'm going out, so don't stop stirring that spell until I get back, right?"

"Yes, mistress," came Mittens' frightened voice.

"Off we go, broom. I want to find that dragon, Flame," the witch said, and chuckled evilly. "I've got just the spell I want to try out on him. It's about time he learned what witches are really made of – and that Spooky Wood is mine!"

As soon as Hannah heard the witch's broomstick going, she raced over to the cave to see Mittens. But suddenly, the

broom screeched, "Mistress, mistress! There's another cat down there. I saw it!"

Hannah darted behind a tree, just before the witch looked down.

"What! I can't see anything!" she exclaimed. "Don't be silly, broom!"

"But I did, I know I did!"

"Well, you must have been mistaken!"

Their voices faded into the distance. Hannah grinned to herself, then she ran to the cave and went inside.

"Mittens! Are you all right?" Hannah called out to her.

Mittens looked up and started in amazement.

"Oh, Hannah!" she cried. "I thought I'd never see you again!" Mittens embraced her, and kissed her on the nose.

Hannah beamed at her.

"I've found you at last!" she said. "Now we've got to stop that witch. She's going to put a spell on Flame, the dragon! But how can we do it?"

"I know how!" said Mittens, excitedly. "The witch forgot her wand when she went out."

"How does that help?" asked Hannah.

"Well, we'll get the key to the cupboard where the witch keeps her wand, then we can hide and when she comes back, we can jump out and send her, by magic, to Timbuctoo, or somewhere like that!"

"Good for you, Mittens!" said Hannah. "But where's the key?"

"Here!" said Mittens, leading the way to a corner of the cavern. There was an old

black bag there. She fumbled around in it and brought out a small golden key.

"Here it is!" she said. The two cats went back to the cupboard. Mittens unlocked it and there, in a small dark space, was the wand. It was shiny, and it was plain that it

was very powerful.

"Quick!" said Hannah. "I think I can hear the witch coming back!"

Hurriedly, Mittens grabbed the wand and shut the cupboard door. She didn't have time to lock it, so she dropped the key on the ground. She and Hannah darted behind the cupboard. They were just in time!

A moment later, the witch came in, grumbling and shouting for Mittens as usual.

"Mittens! Mittens! Where is that stupid cat? Mittens!"

The witch was very cross

indeed. She'd forgotten her wand and without it her spells were useless. As she went by the cupboard, she noticed the key.

"I wonder how the key got there?" she exclaimed.

As she was puzzling over it, Mittens and Hannah crept out and surprised the witch. Mittens pointed the wand at her and shouted as loudly as she could,

"Abracadabra, fiddely doon,
Take this witch up to the moon,
Let her stay for ever and ever,
And make her not so very clever!"

There was a flash of
lightning, and everything
disappeared. The cats hid their
eyes for fear of being blinded.
When they opened them, they

found themselves almost at the
end of Spooky Wood and
Mittens no longer held the
wand in her paw.

"Hurrah!" cried Mittens.
"That's got rid of her."

They ate their blackbird
sandwiches and scratched a
hurried message on a leaf:

Dear Lily and Flame,
please get together
with your families and
friends, and bring them
to the cats' school,
in the old stables.

Love from
Hannah
X X X X

5.
Home at Last!

After a long walk, Mittens and Hannah finally arrived at the old stables. The whole school was assembled. Mr Soots, the big, black tom, who was the headmaster, had been very anxious when Hannah and Mittens had not come in after break-time the day before with the rest of the cats. He had sent for Smokey and Melinda who had told him all

they knew. Now Mr Soots was
saying, "If Hannah and
Mittens do not come back
soon, we . . ."

Suddenly he was interrupted.
Melinda, who was sitting by
the door, watching for them,
shrieked:

"There they are!"

Everyone ran outside and shouted, "Where have you been?"

Mr Soots picked them both up and said, "Let's go inside and you can tell us the whole story!"

So Hannah told the tale, with Mittens putting in the bits that Hannah forgot.

When Hannah had finished, Mittens caught sight of a strange procession.

"What on earth . . ." she thought. "Oh, of course! It's the dragons and the fairies!" She nudged Hannah and pointed.

"Silence! Shhhhhhhhhhh!"
shouted Hannah.

Immediately, everybody
"shushed".

"I have something else to tell

you! Before we came back, I sent a message to Lily and Flame asking them to bring all their friends and to come here. I would like to have a party but where are we going to get all the party food and balloons and things like that?"

Suddenly, Miss Ping and Miss Leo stood up, smiling.

"While you were telling your story we prepared a small welcome home dinner for you! Come and see!"

Hannah and Mittens followed Miss Ping and Miss Leo outside.

What a sight met their eyes!

There was a big rectangular table loaded with food and drink. There was also a big banner tied between two trees,

saying: "WELCOME
HOME MITTENS AND
HANNAH!!!" There were
balloons and streamers of
every shape, size and colour.
 All the other cats, kittens

and teachers came racing out
into the sunshine. Just then, the
dragons and fairies came up
with Flame and Lily leading
them.

"Hi! Come and sit down!"

said Mittens. Sootica, one of
Mittens' friends, said,

"I know! Let's have some
music on!"

Smokey said, "Yes, put on 'I
should be a pussy'!"

"No!" said Flame. "That's a
load of rubbish! Let's have,
'It's no dragon'!"

"Not on your nelly, Flame!"
cried Lily. "Let's put on 'I
heard a fairy'!"

Mr Soots shouted, "All right,
all right! I'm going to put on,
first, 'I heard a fairy', second,
'It's no dragon', and third, 'I
should be a pussy'!"

Mr Soots put on the music

and everyone started dancing,
except Hannah. Mr Soots
walked up to her.

"What's the matter? Why
aren't you dancing?" he asked.

"I'm sorry, Mr Soots, but
I've just thought of
something."

The head looked puzzled.

"What?" he enquired.

"I've forgotten to invite one of my friends. It's Winnie Wildcat. She's the one who told me where Mittens was. It's not fair for her to miss all the fun!"

Mr Soots smiled, and said, "I think I can arrange that."

Hannah looked relieved. "Can you, Mr Soots? Thank you so much!"

And, sure enough, Winnie was soon there, joining in the fun and games. After they had eaten, they played some more party games. Mr Soots said they needn't come back the next day, because it was a special holiday.

Hannah and Mittens went home and their owners, Dan and Becky, were very relieved to see them. They thought the cats had been lost for ever.

"Where have you been?" Becky asked. Of course, the

cats couldn't reply, but they mewed instead. Then they winked at each other.

That night a cat-sized parcel came through the cat-flap, just before Dan had shut it. As he

came into the kitchen, Hannah
quickly hid it under the table.
When Dan had gone, they
opened it and found that it was
two gold trophies with a picture
of the Great Cat on the front of
each. On the trophies it said,
"Awarded for great bravery",
and there was a note which
read:

Thank you for saving
Spooky Wood from
the witch.
    Love,
        Flame and Lily
            X X X

Hannah and Mittens kept their trophies proudly and polished them every day. And they never had any problems with witches again.